Anansi and the Bag of Wisdom

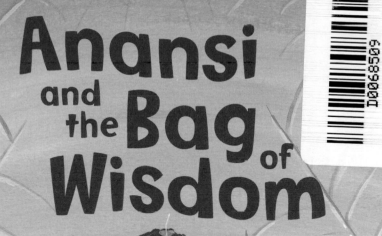

Lesley Sims

Illustrated by Alida Massari

Reading consultant: Alison Kelly
Roehampton University

Anansi was king of
the spiders.

One day, a god gave
him a present.

"This bag has all the wisdom in the world.

Anansi, you
must share it."

Anansi frowned. He didn't want to share it.

"I must hide the bag,"
he thought.

He found the tallest tree in the jungle...

...and started
to climb.

But the bag got
in the way.

His son tried to help.

"But I have the bag of wisdom," Anansi said.

"I should know it
goes on my back."

19

He threw the bag
down into a bush.

It burst open.

Wisdom flew all
over the world.

Everyone had some.

Now everyone knows something...

...but no one knows
everything.

PUZZLES

Puzzle 1
Can you match the opposites?

open

happy

tall

shut

sad

short

Puzzle 2
Choose the best speech
bubble for each picture.

Puzzle 3
Can you spot the differences
between these two pictures?

There are six to find.

Answers to puzzles

Puzzle 1

open

shut

tall

short

sad

happy

Puzzle 2

Put it on your back.

Oh no!

About Anansi

Anansi, the trickster spider, is a popular character in lots of West African and Caribbean folktales. In some stories, he appears as a man, or half-man, half-spider.

Designed by Louise Flutter
Series designer: Russell Punter
Digital manipulation: John Russell

First published in 2011 by Usborne Publishing Ltd., Usborne House,
83-85 Saffron Hill, London EC1N 8RT, England. www.usborne.com
Copyright © 2011 Usborne Publishing Ltd.